2/06

W9-BZC-848

THIS BLOOMSBURY BOOK

BELONGS TO

....

For Stephen and Liz Baird,
with many thanks – SG

For Paulina, Mary Elizabeth,
Dorothy and Valentina McNeill – ET

First published in Great Britain in 2002
First published in the United States of America in 2002
This edition published in 2004

Text copyright © 2002 by Sally Grindley
Illustrations copyright © 2002 by Eleanor Taylor

Published by Bloomsbury, New York and London
Distributed to the trade by Holtzbrinck Publishers

Library of Congress Cataloging-in-Publication Data
Grindley, Sally.
No trouble at all / by Sally Grindley ; illustrated by Eleanor Taylor.
p. cm.
Summary: Grandfather Bear thinks his cubs are so wonderful,
he cannot imagine them being naughty.
ISBN 1-58234-757-3 (hardcover)
ISBN 1-58234-894-4 (paperback)
[1. Grandfathers—Fiction. 2. Sleepovers—Fiction. 3. Behavior—Fiction.
4. Bears—Fiction] I. Taylor, Eleanor 1969-, ill. II. Title.
PZ7.G88446 No 2002
[E]—dc21
2001043982

Printed in Belgium by Proost
1 3 5 7 9 10 8 6 4 2

Bloomsbury USA Children's Books
175 Fifth Avenue
New York, NY 10010

No Trouble at All

by Sally Grindley
illustrated by Eleanor Taylor

BLOOMSBURY
CHILDREN'S
BOOKS

Shhh! They're fast asleep.
Don't wake them up.

They're such good little
bears when they come
to stay.

I just have to say it's time
for bed, and off they go,
as good as gold.

When I was their age
I was full of mischief.

These old houses are full of strange noises.
I'd better just check those little bears
aren't frightened.

Not a sound.
I must have worn
them out.

I'll just fetch
my slippers.

Ah, here they are.

Their mother says those little bears can be very naughty. I'm sure that can't be true.

What was that?

I guess I didn't close the door
properly. Silly of me.

It's a beautiful night.
If it's sunny tomorrow
we'll all go for a picnic.

I'll just fetch
the picnic basket
from the shed.

Here we are. Tomorrow
I'll fill it with sandwiches
and cakes and chocolates and
drinks and off we'll go.

They deserve a treat, those little bears. They're absolutely no trouble.

No trouble at all.

Now available:

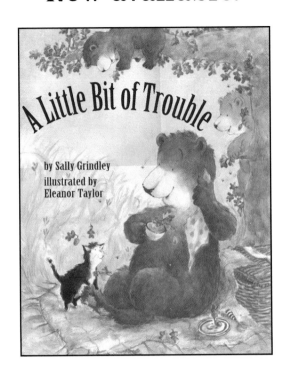

The next story about these delightful cubs and their grandfather!

Sally Grindley

has written more than fifty books for children, including *Mucky Duck* and *Spilled Water*. She lives in Gloucestershire, England, with her husband, three sons, and two cats.

Eleanor Taylor

studied architecture and later moved to Spain to paint murals. She has illustrated several books for children, including *Tick-Tock, Drip-Drop!* by Nicola Moon. She lives in London, England.

OXFORD FREE LIBRARY
339 Main Street
Oxford, Ma. 01540